DINOSAUR

**Written by
John Malam**

DK

Reptile World

Millions of years ago, planet Earth was ruled by reptiles. There were reptiles in the sky and in the sea, and on the land lived the best-known reptiles of all—the ones we call dinosaurs. But what, exactly, were dinosaurs?

Meet a Dinosaur

An animal can only be a dinosaur if it is all of the following things. It must have lived between 250 and 65 million years ago, and only on dry land—not in the sky or the sea. It must have had four limbs and walked on upright legs, not on sprawling legs like a crocodile. And it must have laid eggs and had scales or feathers on its skin. Put all these together, and you get a dinosaur!

Dinosaur Families

About 1,000 different species (kinds) of dinosaur have been found and named. They can be divided into family groups.

Ceratopsians:
dinosaurs with horns

Sauropods:
big plant-eaters

Theropods:
meat-eaters

Ankylosaurs:
armored dinosaurs

Pachycephalosaurs:
bone-headed dinosaurs

Stegosaurs:
dinosaurs with bony
plates or spikes

Not Dinosaurs

Other reptiles lived at the very same time as dinosaurs. These reptiles spent all or most of their lives flying or swimming, not living on dry land. Pterosaurs flew on leathery wings, while mosasaurs, plesiosaurs, pliosaurs, and ichthyosaurs swam in the sea. They were totally different from dinosaurs because they could fly and swim. Among the fliers was Pterodactylus, while the swimmers included Icthyosaurus, Elasmosaurus, and Kronosaurus.

3

Age of Dinosaurs

Dinosaurs lived on Earth for a very long time. From start to finish they were here for about 185 million years. This was a time in Earth's history called the Mesozoic Era, which is also known as the Age of Dinosaurs. Earth was very different then from the planet we know today.

EARTH TODAY

Today, Earth is made up of seven continents, five oceans, and many seas. It hasn't always been like this.

Sections (plates) of Earth's crust are constantly moving.

Coelophysis

Shifting Continents

Way back at the start of the Age of Dinosaurs (that's 250 million years ago), there was just one big supercontinent called Pangaea. The name means "All Earth," because all the planet's land was joined together. Over millions of years, the supercontinent broke up into smaller continents. Very slowly, they moved across the face of the Earth. By the end of the Age of Dinosaurs (65 million years ago), the continents had just about reached the positions they are in today.

Pangaea

In the Beginning

Travel back to the start of the Age of Dinosaurs, to a time known as the Triassic period. This was when the very first dinosaurs appeared—small two-legged meat-eaters, and larger plant-eaters that walked on two or four legs. Because all of Earth's land was joined together in a giant land-mass, the first dinosaurs were free to wander in any direction they liked, since there were no oceans to get in their way.

Eoraptor

Triassic Period (250–206 million years ago)

Jurassic Period (206–

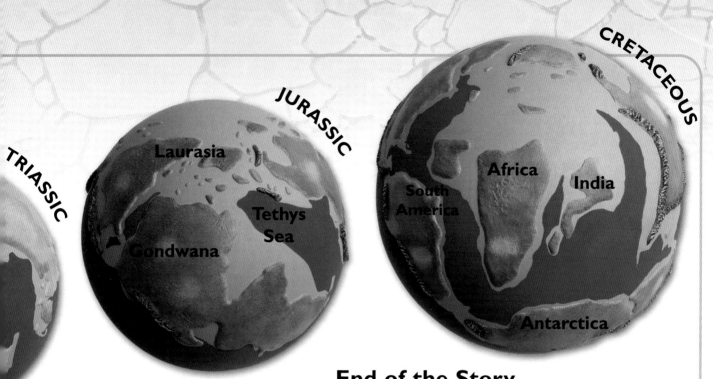

Laurasia

Tethys
Sea

Gondwana

South
America

Africa

India

Antarctica

What Happened Next?

The middle part of the Age of Dinosaurs is
known as the Jurassic period. During this
time the supercontinent began to break up
into smaller continents. Cracks opened up
in the Earth's crust, and seawater flooded in
to form oceans. Dinosaurs could no longer
travel freely across the whole planet.
They lived on the new continents, and
over time each continent developed its
very own dinosaurs.

End of the Story

The final part of the Age of Dinosaurs is a time
known as the Cretaceous period. The continents had
more or less moved to their present-day positions,
and each one was stocked with its own species of
dinosaurs—including Antarctica, which wasn't a
frozen place like it is today. There were plant-eaters
that lived in huge herds, and meat-eaters that
hunted in packs or on their own. There were
hundreds of different dinosaurs, and yet,
at the end of the Cretaceous period,
they died out.

Tyrannosaurus rex

Velociraptor

Diplodocus

5

40 million years ago)

Cretaceous Period (140–65 million years ago)

Dinosaur Time

The Age of Dinosaurs was a time of many changes. Not only did the continents slowly shift their positions around the world, but the environment changed, too. It varied from hot and dry to cool and wet, and as the conditions changed, new kinds of trees and plants appeared.

Triassic World

All through the Triassic period, the temperature on land was dry and warm. Near the coast were lush forests, where trees such as conifers and ginkgoes grew. Ferns, horsetails, and cycads grew at ground level.

The world's first dinosaurs, such as Eoraptor and Coelophysis, lived in this environment, but away from the coast it was a different story. The center of Pangaea was a hot, dry desert, where dinosaurs rarely ventured.

Ginkgo tree and leaves

Conifer tree

Coelophysis

Horsetail plant and stand

Tree fern

Eoraptor

6

Jurassic World

The environment changed in the Jurassic period, as Pangaea began to break up into smaller pieces. The temperature became cooler, rainfall increased, and the air changed from dry to moist. Shallow seas surrounded the land, deserts shrank, the conifer forests and plants such as ginkgoes, tree ferns, and horsetails spread. The world became a dinosaur park, in which Diplodocus and other giant plant-eaters fed on the lush vegetation.

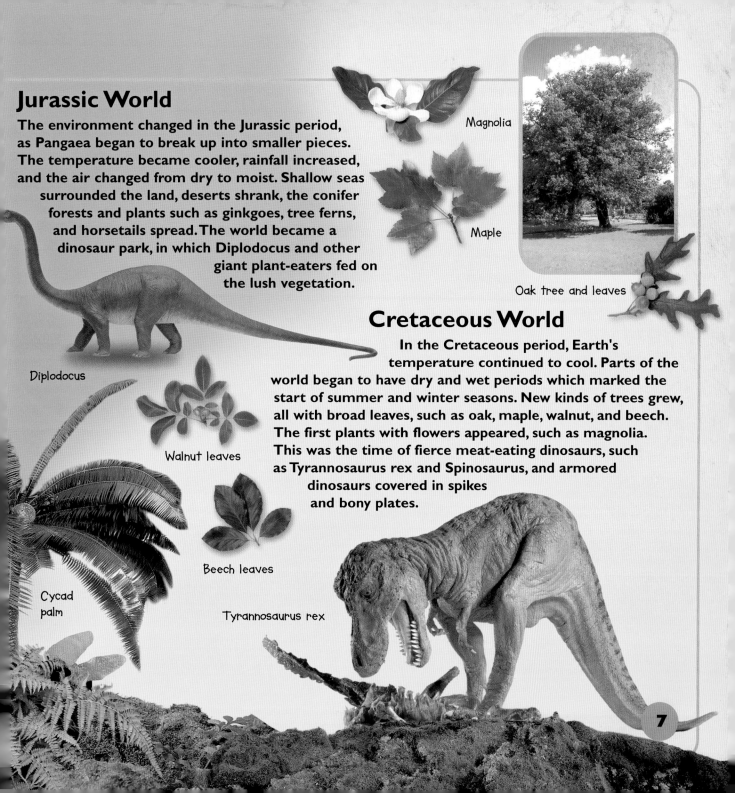

Magnolia

Maple

Oak tree and leaves

Diplodocus

Cretaceous World

In the Cretaceous period, Earth's temperature continued to cool. Parts of the world began to have dry and wet periods which marked the start of summer and winter seasons. New kinds of trees grew, all with broad leaves, such as oak, maple, walnut, and beech. The first plants with flowers appeared, such as magnolia. This was the time of fierce meat-eating dinosaurs, such as Tyrannosaurus rex and Spinosaurus, and armored dinosaurs covered in spikes and bony plates.

Walnut leaves

Beech leaves

Cycad palm

Tyrannosaurus rex

7

Gentle Giants

Some dinosaurs became giants. Many of the biggest dinosaurs belonged to a group known as sauropods. The sauropods were the tallest, longest, and heaviest animals that have ever walked on Earth.

Super-Sized Sauropods

The sauropods were big and heavy and they walked on all four legs. Sauropod dinosaurs were plant-eaters (herbivores), with long necks and long tails, but rather small heads. Their teeth were blunt and shaped like pegs, which was the best shape for stripping leaves and pine needles from the branches of trees. Just like today's leaf-eating animals, sauropods probably had to keep eating all day long, just to stay alive.

Imagine being able to reach leaves that grew 50 ft (15 m) off the ground! That's what an adult Brachiosaurus could do when its long neck stretched up into the trees.

Jurassic Giraffe

No wonder Brachiosaurus has been called the giraffe of the dinosaur world! As well as leaves growing at the tops of trees, Brachiosaurus ate plants that grew down on the ground. It needed to eat about 440 lb (200 kg) of plants every single day to keep its massive body healthy.

Brachiosaurus:
Say: brak-ee-oh-sore-us
Name means: "Arm Lizard"
Diet: Plants
Lived: 150 million years ago
Found: North America;
Africa; Europe
Length: 82 ft (25 m)
Weight: 30-50 tons

Big Eater

Diplodocus had a really long neck and tail. Its neck was 25 ft (8 m) long, and its tail stretched for 45 ft (14 m). Like all sauropods, Diplodocus did not chew its food. It gulped down leaves and twigs, which were crushed to bits inside its stomach by stones it had swallowed. These stones, which are called "gastroliths," rolled against the plants and crushed them to a mushy pulp that Diplodocus could digest.

Diplodocus skeleton

Diplodocus:

Say: die–ploh–de–kus
Name means: "Double Beam Lizard"
Diet: Plants
Lived: 150 million years ago
Found: North America
Length: 88 ft (27 m)
Weight: 12 tons

Earth-Shaker

The ground really would have trembled each time Seismosaurus went for a stroll. This giant among giants also had an incredibly long neck with a tiny head perched at the end. Its long tail narrowed to a thin end. If it was attacked, it may have used its tail like a whip, flicking it at its enemy to scare it away.

Seismosaurus:

Say: size–moh–sore–us
Name means: "Earth-Shaking Lizard"
Diet: Plants
Lived: 150 million years ago
Found: North America
Length: 130 ft (40 m)
Weight: 60 tons

A Diplodocus herd with young and old animals all together.

Killers!

Their jaws were packed with razor-sharp teeth. They had good eyesight, a keen sense of smell, and could run fast. These were the theropods—a group of dinosaurs that included some of the most ferocious animals ever to live on Earth.

Terrifying Theropods

The theropods were meat-eaters (carnivores). They moved quickly on two legs. Some, like Compsognathus, were only about the size of a hen, but others were huge. They hunted their prey in packs, as well as on their own. Theropods could also be scavengers, which means they ate meat from animals that were already dead. A plant-eating dinosaur could be the target for a hungry meat-eater. Theropods attacked their victims quickly, ripping at their flesh with sharp teeth and pointed claws.

Dilophosaurus was a fast moving theropod. The crest on its head was probably just for display.

Tyrannosaurus rex:
Say: tie-ran-oh-sore-us
Name means: "King of the Tyrant Lizards'"
Diet: Meat
Lived: 70 million years ago
Found: North America
Length: 40 ft (12 m)
Weight: 7 tons

Massive Meat-Eater

Tyrannosaurus rex is probably the world's best-known dinosaur. It had the power of speed, and could chase its prey at up to 22 mph (36 km/h). Each giant stride of its legs covered about 13 ft (4 m).

A Tyrannosaurus rex's tooth could be up to 8 in (20 cm) long.

Tyranno-teeth

When it bit into its prey, Tyrannosaurus rex's knifelike teeth sliced deep into the victim's flesh. Then it tugged its head from side to side, tearing off a chunk of meat and bone that could weigh as much as 500 lb (230 kg)—that's about the weight of three sheep! After eating, Tyrannosaurus rex probably went for several days before needing to eat again.

Gigantic Meat-eater

For many years, Tyrannosaurus rex was the biggest meat-eating dinosaur ever found. But then Giganotosaurus was discovered, and it turned out to be even bigger. Just like other giant meat-eaters, its biting teeth had serrated (jagged) edges. This made the cutting edge really good for slicing through skin, flesh, muscle, and bone. Giganotosaurus lived in South America, alongside giant sauropods such as Argentinosaurus, which it may have hunted. These massive herbivores would have been many times bigger than Giganotosaurus, and hard to kill. Giganotosaurus probably wounded its prey, and waited for it to bleed to death before starting to eat it.

Giganotosaurus:
Say: jig-an-oh-toe-sore-rus
Name means: "Giant Southern Lizard"
Diet: Meat
Lived: 100 million years ago
Found: South America
Length: 52 ft (16 m)
Weight: 8 tons

Hunters

Some carnivores hunted in packs, but others acted alone. **No matter how they caught their prey, one thing is clear—meat-eating dinosaurs were born to hunt. They were the ultimate predators of the dinosaur age.**

No Escape

Dinosaurs that hunted for food needed to track down their prey using senses. **Once they had found it, they needed to catch it and kill it.** They were fast movers with strong, muscular bodies. These hunter-killers chased after their victims, which they attacked and killed with their sharp teeth and claws.

Big Bite

Long before Tyrannosaurus rex roamed the world, Allosaurus was the largest predator on the planet. It lived alongside plant-eaters such as Diplodocus, Camptosaurus, and Stegosaurus, all of which it might have hunted. Allosaurus would have used all of its senses to detect its prey. Once it had found its victim, Allosaurus closed in for the kill. When Allosaurus bit into its victim, its jaws opened really wide so it could bite off a huge chunk of flesh.

Allosaurus:
Say: al-oh-sore-us
Name means: "Different Lizard"
Diet: Meat
Lived: 140 million years ago
Found: North America
Length: 40 ft (12 m)
Weight: 4 tons

Allosaurus attacking Diplodocus.

Velociraptors attacking a Protoceratops. Fossils of these two species have been found locked in combat.

ALLOSAURUS FACTS

• Its eyes faced forward to give it a good sense of vision.

• It probably had a good sense of smell and hearing.

• Inside its jaws were many backward pointing teeth, some of which were 4 in (10 cm) long.

• The claws at the ends of its fingers were perfect for slashing. Each were up to 6 in (15 cm) long.

Pack Hunter

It might have been one of the smaller meat-eaters, but size didn't matter to Velociraptor. It was a fast-moving predator that was clever enough to hunt in packs. Once a pack had caught up with its prey, such as a Protoceratops, the end came quickly. Each Velociraptor kicked at the prey, hoping to slash through its skin with long, curved claws on its hind feet. Its claws were sharp enough to pierce the toughest skin. As its feet kicked away, Velociraptor gripped its victim with its hands and bit at it with its sharp teeth.

13

Dinosaur Defenses

Plant-eating dinosaurs were animals in danger. They were attacked and eaten by hungry meat-eaters. For their own protection, some plant-eaters came up with clever ways of defending themselves.

Euoplocephalus was so well protected, that even its eyelids had a layer of bone over them!

Body Armor

One group of plant-eaters protected their bodies with armor. These were the ankylosaurs, or armored dinosaurs. Hard, bony plates, knobs, and spikes covered their bodies, making it difficult for a carnivore to attack them. Some ankylosaurs, like Euoplocephalus, grew heavy, bony clubs at the ends of their tails. If attacked, it swung its tail club from side to side, warning a predator to keep away.

Euoplocephalus:
Say: yoo-op-loh-sef-ah-lus
Name means: "Well Armored Head"
Diet: Plants
Lived: 70 million years ago
Found: North America
Length: 20 ft (6 m)
Weight: 2 tons

Horn Face!

Having horns, like a modern-day rhinoceros, was another good form of defense. Dinosaurs with horns are called ceratopsians. They were plant-eaters with horns on their faces and bony shields at the backs of their heads. The biggest horned dinosaur was Triceratops. It had three long horns on its face If Triceratops was attacked, its horns would easily go through skin and flesh, causing a lot of damage to its enemy.

Triceratops:
Say: try-ser-ah-tops
Name means: "Three-Horned Face"
Diet: Plants
Lived: 70 million years ago
Found: North America
Length: 30 ft (9 m)
Weight: 5 tons

Spiny!

One group of dinosaurs had rows of upright bony plates on their backs. These were the stegosaurs, or plated dinosaurs. They also had sharp spines on their tails and bodies. The best-known stegosaur was Stegosaurus. It was a slow mover and could not run away from an attacker. If a meat-eater, such as Allosaurus, attacked Stegosaurus, it defended itself by swinging its spiky tail.

The spikes on the end of Stegosaurus's tail could be more than 3 ft (1 m) long.

Stegosaurus:
Say: ste-go-sore-us
Name means: "Roofed Lizard"
Diet: Plants
Lived: 140 million years ago
Found: North America
Length: 30 ft (9 m)
Weight: 2 tons

Stegosaurus had to eat lots of plants to grow so big, but what ate Stegosaurus? Probably hungry meat-eaters like this Allosaurus!

15

Dinosaur Babies

Just like the reptiles of today—crocodiles, turtles, lizards, and snakes, dinosaurs laid eggs. It might seem incredible to believe, but thousands of dinosaur eggs have been found all over the world, and some of them were still in their nests!

Nest and Eggs

Maiasaura was a plant-eater that lived on high ground overlooking the sea. It was a hadrosaur, or duck-billed dinosaur, and it lived in herds. At breeding time, the Maiasaura dinosaurs chose a good place to make their nests. Each nest was made on the ground, and was about 6 ft (2 m) across. The nest was lined with plant material to make it soft, and then a clutch of up to 25 eggs was laid inside. Each egg was oval in shape and was about the size of a grapefruit.

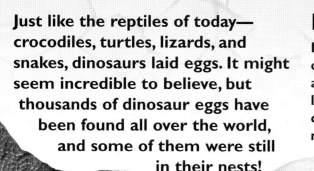

Egg with baby dinosaur inside.

Maiasaura watching over eggs in a nest.

Hatching Out

After the eggs had been laid, Maiasaura covered them with a thick layer of plants. As the plants rotted, they made heat, and this was how the eggs were kept warm. Maiasaura stayed by the nest, guarding it from eggs-thieves. The name Maiasaura actually means "good mother." No one knows how long it took the eggs to hatch, but when they did, the new babies were about 12 in (30 cm) long.

A Maiasaura egg hatching.

This dinosaur egg fossil is from Mongolia.

Growing Up

Maiasaura babies probably stayed with their parents for a few years, until they were old enough to look after themselves. By the age of about 10 years, they were fully grown, and that's when they could start families of their own.

Sitting on her Nest

For many years, scientists thought Oviraptor was an egg thief, which is how it got its name. This was because it was found with a clutch of eggs, which scientists thought it was stealing! It turns out the eggs actually belonged to Oviraptor. This dinosaur laid about 20 eggs in a nest scraped in the sand, then sat on them to keep them warm, just like a bird.

Weird and Wonderful

Dinosaurs were remarkable animals, and it's amazing how much we actually know about them even though they died out millions of years ago. By studying their fossilized bones, it's possible to work out exactly what they looked like—and even how brainy they were (or not)!

Big Brain

Troodon was a small, fast-moving meat-eater with a bigger brain and more biting teeth in its mouth than any other carnivore. It might have been one of the brainiest of all dinosaurs, but if it were alive today, Troodon wouldn't seem that bright. In fact, scientists think Troodon had about the same brain power as a pig, which isn't very much at all!

Bone Head

Pachycephalosaurus was the largest of the bone-heads—a group of dinosaurs with extra thick skulls. The bone that formed the top of its skull was an incredible 10 in (25 cm) thick! It must have been thick for a good reason. If Pachycephalosaurus was attacked, it head-butted its enemy, hurting it and knocking it off balance.

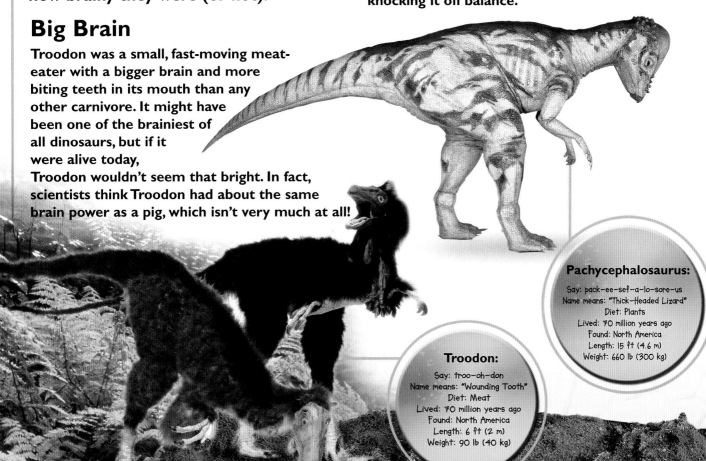

Pachycephalosaurus:
Say: pack-ee-sef-a-lo-sore-us
Name means: "Thick-Headed Lizard"
Diet: Plants
Lived: 70 million years ago
Found: North America
Length: 15 ft (4.6 m)
Weight: 660 lb (300 kg)

Troodon:
Say: troo-oh-don
Name means: "Wounding Tooth"
Diet: Meat
Lived: 70 million years ago
Found: North America
Length: 6 ft (2 m)
Weight: 90 lb (40 kg)

Parrot Beak

Psittacosaurus did not have any teeth in the front of its mouth. Instead, it had a horny beak that looked a bit like the beak of a parrot. When Psittacosaurus bit down, its beak could slice through the toughest of plants. Its tongue pushed the plants to the back of its mouth, where lots of small chewing teeth crushed them to bits.

Psittacosaurus:
Say: sit-ak-oh-sore-us
Name means: "Parrot Lizard"
Diet: Plants
Lived: 130 million years ago
Found: Asia
Length: 8 ft (2.5 m)
Weight: 110 lb (50 kg)

Parasaurolophus:
Say: sit-ak-oh-sore-us
Name means: "Beside Saurolophus"
Diet: Plants
Lived: 75 million years ago
Found: North America
Length: 33 ft (10 m)
Weight: 3.5 tons

Trumpet Head

The most obvious thing about Parasaurolophus was the long, bony crest on the top of its head. It was a hollow tube connected to its throat. Parasaurolophus could blow air through the tube, making a trumpeting noise. Just like today's animals, Parasaurolophus probably had a range of calls, from friendly ones to ones that warned of danger.

Masters of the Seas and Skies

While dinosaurs ruled the land, other reptiles controlled the sea and the sky. In the world's oceans were animals built for speed and hunting, and in the skies above were flying creatures whose leathery wings carried them far and wide.

Pterosaurs

All through the Age of Dinosaurs, winged reptiles filled the skies. These were the pterosaurs, or "wing-lizards." Their wings were made from thin sheets of skin that stretched along their arms. Many different species existed, from pterosaurs with tiny wingspans to Quetzalcoatlus, which was the biggest creature that has ever flown.

Hunters of the Deep

Just like dinosaurs, sea-dwelling reptiles had scaly skin, some laid eggs on the beach (like turtles), and they breathed air. They had to come to the surface to fill their lungs and held their breath as they swam underwater. Some may have been able to detect underwater scent, as sharks do today. In an environment where visibility was poor, being able to smell was a big advantage.

Quetzalcoatlus:
Say: ket-zal-co-at-luss
Name means: "Feathered Serpent"
Diet: Molluscs; crabs; carrion
Lived: 70 million years ago
Found: North America
Wingspan: 36 ft (11 m)
Weight: 300 lb (135 kg)

Plesiosaurs and Pliosaurs

To tell the difference between a plesiosaur and a pliosaur, look at its neck. Plesiosaurs had long necks; pliosaurs had short ones. Elasmosaurus (right) was a plesiosaur, and Liopleurodon (below) was the biggest pliosaur. This massive reptile was also the biggest meat-eater that has ever lived on Earth! Ever! If Tyrannosaurus rex was king on land, Liopleurodon was king of the sea.

Liopleurodon:
Say: lie-oh-ploor-oh-don
Name means: "Smooth-Sided Tooth"
Diet: Fish; marine reptiles
Lived: 150 million years ago
Found: Europe; South America
Length: 82 ft (25 m)
Weight: 100 tons

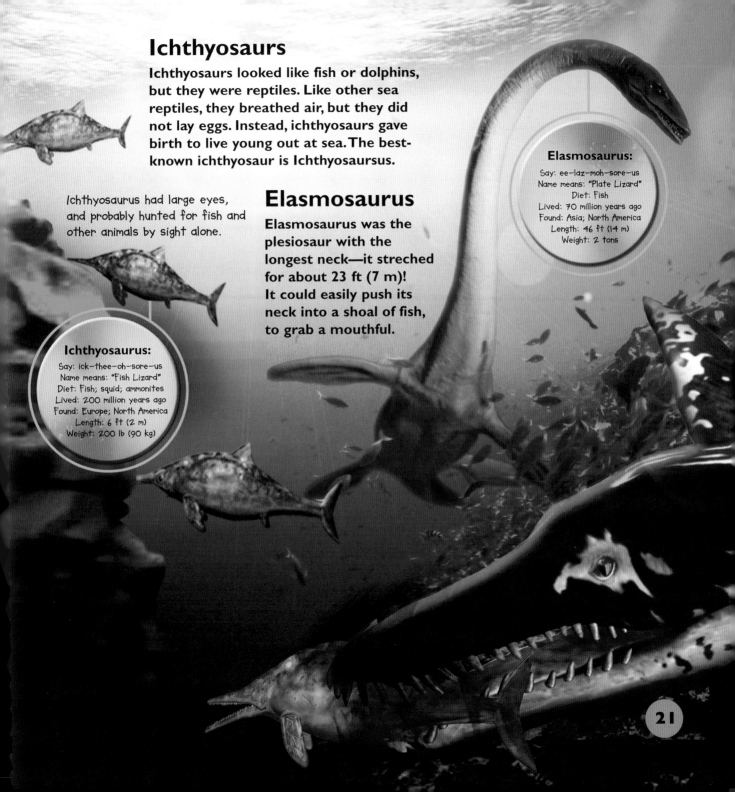

Ichthyosaurs

Ichthyosaurs looked like fish or dolphins, but they were reptiles. Like other sea reptiles, they breathed air, but they did not lay eggs. Instead, ichthyosaurs gave birth to live young out at sea. The best-known ichthyosaur is Ichthyosaursus.

Ichthyosaurus had large eyes, and probably hunted for fish and other animals by sight alone.

Elasmosaurus

Elasmosaurus was the plesiosaur with the longest neck—it streched for about 23 ft (7 m)! It could easily push its neck into a shoal of fish, to grab a mouthful.

Elasmosaurus:
Say: ee-laz-moh-sore-us
Name means: "Plate Lizard"
Diet: Fish
Lived: 70 million years ago
Found: Asia; North America
Length: 46 ft (14 m)
Weight: 2 tons

Ichthyosaurus:
Say: ick-thee-oh-sore-us
Name means: "Fish Lizard"
Diet: Fish; squid; ammonites
Lived: 200 million years ago
Found: Europe; North America
Length: 6 ft (2 m)
Weight: 200 lb (90 kg)

End of an Era

The Age of Dinosaurs came to a sudden end about 65 million years ago. All the dinosaurs, together with the reptiles in the sky and the sea, died out. They became extinct. The big question is: what happened?

Big Bang

Did the dinosaurs die because a meteorite (a space rock) hit the Earth? A big lump of rock, about 6 miles (10 km) across, did smash into the Earth (near present-day Mexico), and could be the reason the dinosaurs died out. It would have caused earthquakes, tidal waves, and fires. And it would have sent a huge cloud of dust into the atmosphere, blotting out sunlight and making the planet dark and cold for a long time.

The meteorite made a huge crater.

Climate Change

Whatever it was that killed the dinosaurs, one thing is clear—the climate changed. For most of the Age of Dinosaurs the climate had been warm, but at the end it became cooler and more changeable. If plants and animals could not survive in this new, cooler world, they died out.

Violent Volcanoes

Was it a volcano? At the same time as the meteorite strike, lots of volcanoes were erupting in present-day India. They blew huge clouds of ash into the atmosphere, making it harder for the Sun's light and heat to reach the ground. The days became dark, and the air was filled with poisonous sulfur fumes. These changes would have made it hard for dinosaurs to survive.

Caudipteryx:
Say: caw–dip–ter–iks
Name means: "Tail Feather"
Diet: Meat
Lived: 125 million years ago
Found: Asia
Length: 3 ft (1 m)
Weight: 5 lb (2.5 kg)

Survivors

Actually, some dinosaurs did find a way to survive. They were chicken-sized meat-eaters who, toward the end of the Age of Dinosaurs, started to grow feathers on their bodies. They had begun to evolve (change) into animals that we see around us today—birds. The skeletons of "dinobirds," such as Caudipteryx, are remarkably similar to those of living birds. The dinosaurs died out, but their relatives—the birds—survived.

Fossils

How do we know about dinosaurs? They died out millions of years ago, but we know a lot about them. We know what they looked like, where they lived, what they ate, how they walked, and much more. All of this is possible because of fossils.

What is a Fossil?

A fossil is the remains of an animal, or a plant, that has been preserved. The process of turning something that was once alive into a fossil is called "fossilization." It is a long, slow process, and can take millions of years from start to finish.

Bone to Stone

If a dinosaur died near a river, it might turn into a fossil. The river would wash a layer of mud, sand, or silt over the dead body and bury it. Over time, more and more sediments would be piled on top, burying the dinosaur deeper and deeper. Its soft parts would rot away, until only its skeleton was left. Eventually, its bones changed and were turned into rock. This type of fossil is a true fossil, because it is made from an actual body part.

Trace Fossils

Some fossils do not come from body parts at all, such as footprints. These are called trace fossils. Fossils of dinosaur footprints are really useful. They tell us if a dinosaur lived alone or in a group, if it walked on two legs or four, and how long its strides were. It's also possible to work out how heavy a dinosaur was, and how fast it moved—all from looking at its footprints!

Semi Preservation: this results when just the hard parts are preserved— unaltered.

A paleontologist investigates one fossil in a wall of fossils formed when dinosaurs drowned in the same place.

Trace Fossils: these are fossils that show where an animal has been, such as footprints, nests, or coprolites (which is dung).

Famous Fossil

One of the world's most famous dinosaur fossils was found in 1990, by American fossil-hunter Sue Hendrickson. She was with a team of fossil collectors working in South Dakota when she came across the best Tyrannosaurus rex skeleton ever found. About 200 bones were dug up, and when they were pieced together they made a nearly complete Tyrannosaurus skeleton. The dinosaur was given the name "Sue," in honour of Sue Hendrickson.

Tyrannosaurus rex "Sue"– the largest and most complete Tyrannosaurus rex skeleton ever found.

Sue at a Glance

Age: Fully grown adult
Length: 42 ft (12.8 m)
Height at hips: 13 ft (4 m)
Live weight: 7 tons
Skull length: 5 ft (1.5 m)
Skull weight: 600 lbs (272 kg)
Number of teeth: 58
Length of teeth: 8-12 in (19–30 cm)
Diet: Meat
Health: Had suffered from broken ribs, a crushed tail, and from an infected jaw
Sex: Thought to be female
Skin color: Unknown
Age at death: Thought to be an old animal
Cause of death: Unknown

Dinosaur Detectives

Today, we know a lot about dinosaurs. We see their bones in museums, read about them in books and on websites, and watch movies and television programs about them. All of this is possible because of the work done by dinosaur detectives.

Richard Owen and the skeleton of an extinct flightless bird

Word Inventor

People have always been curious about fossilized bones. Which animals did they come from? How old were they? Professor Richard Owen worked it all out. He was an expert on animals, and he realized the old bones came from reptiles—but they were not at all like living reptiles. In 1842, Owen invented a new word to describe the animals they came from. The word he used was "dinosaur," which meant "terrible lizard."

Fossil Finders

People who study dinosaur fossils are called paleontologists. They are experts at finding buried fossils and digging them up. If dinosaur bones are in soft ground, such as a sandy desert, they are easy to uncover. Others might be trapped in solid rock, so the fossil finders have to use hammers, chisels, and drills to loosen them. During the excavation they photograph and draw plans (maps) of the bones.

Paleontologists hard at work, uncovering the rest of the Tyrannosaurus rex. The bones were removed one by one.

On Display

When dinosaur bones come out of the ground, they are still trapped in chunks of rock. The rock is carefully chipped away at the museum until the bones are all loose. This can take years to do! The actual bones are very fragile, so exact copies of them are made. The real bones are put away in museum storage, while the copies are joined together and put on display for people to see.

A dinosaur model on a computer screen

Digital Dinosaur

The dinosaur fossils are measured, and all the information is put into a computer. A computer program uses the measurements to create images of the dinosaur. One image will show its skeleton, while another will put flesh and skin back on the bones to show what it looked like when it was a living animal. The computer image can be made to run and walk. By doing all of this, dusty old dinosaur bones come back to life, and we feel we are looking back to the Age of Dinosaurs.

replica bone is made in a mold

27

Model Instructions

Your kit includes four plastic sheets of model pieces that you can use to build your very own glow-in-the-dark Velociraptor model!

Tips to get you started

Lay out the four sheets like the diagram below to make it easy to follow. Use the color key and the numbers marked on the plastic pieces to help you find each piece and match it to its slot. You may need the help of an adult to snap the pieces into their slots correctly. The easiest way to remove a piece from the plastic sheet is by cutting the thin piece of plastic that holds it onto the stem with scissors. Be careful to only cut off each piece as you need it, as the pieces are easily lost.

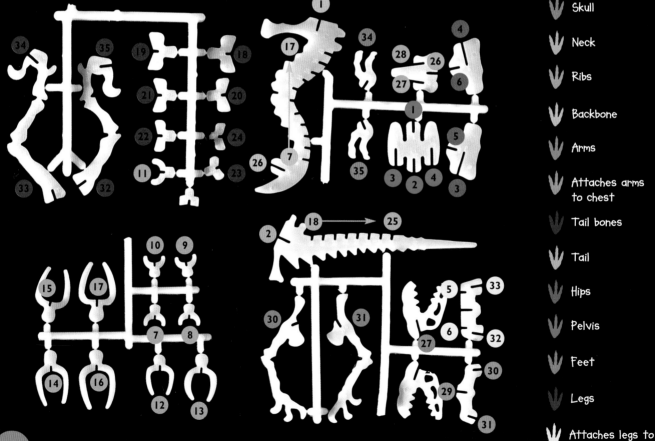

Skull

Neck

Ribs

Backbone

Arms

Attaches arms to chest

Tail bones

Tail

Hips

Pelvis

Feet

Legs

Attaches legs to bottom of pelvis

Tail

Body and neck

Legs and hips

Head

Arms

Build your own spooky skeleton

Join the two skull pieces, 27 and 28, to the neck piece, 26. Join the neck to the top of the backbone.

Detach the rib pieces 7–17 and slot them along the back of the backbone, starting with the smallest at the top and using larger pieces as you progress downward. Note that piece 11 can be found with the tailbone pieces.

Attach each of the arms, pieces 31 and 30, to piece 29, and then attach this section to the slot halfway down the front of the backbone.

Attach the tailbones to the tail, working up from smallest to largest as it gets thicker.

Slot the hip bones, pieces 3 and 4, into the pelvis, piece 1. Attach the backbone, with arms and ribs attached to one side of the pelvis, marked 1, and the tail with tailbones attached to the other side, marked 2, ensuring the two remaining slots in the pelvis point downward.

Attach the feet, pieces 34 and 35, to the legs, pieces 32 and 33, ensuring the claws on each foot face outward.

Then attach the legs to the piece that attaches to the bottom of the pelvis. Slot the bottom of the pelvis with the legs attached underneath into those two last slots. Your model is now complete and ready to stand on its own!

Eerie glow

When you turn out your light at night, your dinosaur model will glow like a ghost from the prehistoric past, lighting up your room with an eerie glow—how cool is that?!

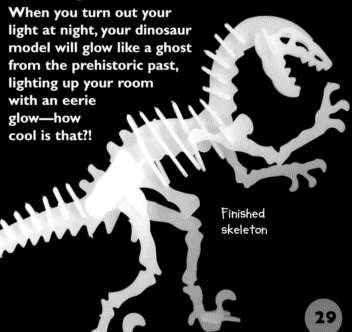

Finished skeleton

Plaster Instructions

Fossils normally form over millions of years, yet your kit includes everything you need to create your very own fossils in only an hour! You can even decorate them in your own designs and colors and keep them to amaze your friends or spruce up your room.

Make your own fossils

1

Pour the 5 oz (125 g) plaster-of-Paris powder into a plastic cup or bowl and add 3 oz (80 ml) of water.

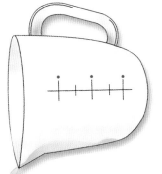

2

Stir thoroughly. Tap the sides of the container to reduce the number of air bubbles. If foam forms on top of the mixture, gently remove it with a spoon.

3 Gently pour the mixture into the molds until they are full.

4

Leave the plaster to dry for an hour.

5

When the plaster is hard, remove the pieces from the molds and decorate them to your own design with the paints provided.

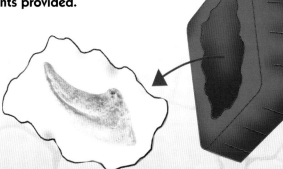

Allosaurus skull

Embedded in stone, this fierce-looking fossilized skull belonged to one of the huge meat-eating dinosaurs of the Jurassic period—Allosaurus. Notice that its rows of sharp teeth curved backward. This angle helped the dinosaur to slash through flesh, not hold onto it.

Ammonite

This swirled fossil shows the shell of an ammonite—an extinct marine animal that lived in the ancient seas throughout the age of the dinosaurs. Most of the ammonite fossils that have been found are fossils of species that were smaller than 9 in (23 cm) in diameter, however, there have been some huge ammonite fossils found that are much larger, up to 7 ft (2 m)!

Tyrannosaurus rex claw

It wasn't just sharp teeth, but also sharp claws that helped meat-eating predators kill their victims. Tyrannosaurus rex had two sharp claws on its small forearms. On its powerful hind legs it had three forward-pointing claws and one backward-pointing one, so it could pierce and slash the skin of its prey with a well-aimed, vicious kick.

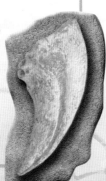

Glossary

Ankylosaur
An armored plant-eating dinosaur covered with bony plates, knobs, and spikes and with a bony club at the end of its tail.

Beak
A horny mouthpart on birds and some dinosaurs. Beaks are used in the same way as teeth, to hold and chop up food.

Carnivore
An animal that eats mainly meat.

Ceratopsian
A large plant-eating dinosaur with pointed horns and a bony frill growing from the back of its skull.

Extinction
Death of every single one of an animal or plant species.

Family
A group of animals or plants which are related to each other.

Fern
A non-flowering plant with finely divided leaves called fronds.

Fossil
The remains of an animal or plant that have been preserved in rock.

Ginkgo
A tree that looks like a conifer but which sheds its leaves in the fall. The only living species of ginkgo is the Maidenhair tree.

Glossary continued...

Gondwana
The southern supercontinent made up of Africa, Australia, Antarctica, South America, and India.

Hadrosaur
A large, plant-eating dinosaur with a long, flat beak.

Herbivore
An animal that only eats plants.

Horsetail
A plant with an upright stem and tiny leaves related to ferns.

Ichthyosaur
A fast-swimming reptile, similar in appearance to a dolphin.

Laurasia
The northern supercontinent made up of North America, Europe, and Asia.

Pachycephalosaur
A two-legged, plant-eating dinosaur with a thick skull.

Paleontologist
A scientist who studies paleontology.

Paleontology
The scientific study of fossils.

Plesiosaur
A swimming reptile that lived in the world's seas during the Jurassic and Cretaceous periods.

Predator
An animal that kills other animals for food.

Prey
Animals hunted and eaten by other animals.

Pterosaur
A flying reptile with wings formed from skin.

Reptile
A cold-blooded animal with scales and a backbone.

Sauropod
A bulky, long-necked, long-tailed plant-eating dinosaur that walked on all four feet.

Sediment
Tiny particles of sand, silt, and clay, deposited in layers by wind, water, or ice.

Theropod
A two-legged, meat-eating dinosaur.

Tyrannosaur
Very large, two-legged, meat-eating dinosaur with short arms.

Dinosaur Discovery Kit Picture Credits

The publisher would like to thank the following for their kind permission to reproduce their photographs:

(Key: a-above; b-below/bottom; c-center; l-left; r-right; t-top)

Ardea: François Gohier 16tr; CM Studio: 4bc, 6bc, 10bl (T-Rex); Corbis: Gary Bell 3, 20bl (sea bed); Layne Kennedy 11tl; Louie Psihoyos 16br, 16cla; Reuters 25b; DK Images: The American Museum of Natural History 27bl; Dinosaur State Park, Connecticut 24crb; Dougal Dixon 18bl; Getty Images: Theo Allofs 4-5bc; Louie Psihoyos 24clb, 26b; James Randklev 5br; Miguel Salmeron 13ca (rocks and grass); Hans Strand 10bl, 11r, 18bl (ferns); The Natural History Museum, London: 16l, 17br, 26tr; John Downs 16cb; Science Faction Images: Louie Psihoyos 24b; Science Photo Library: Christian Darkin 8-9; Bernhard Edmaier 23tl; NASA 22-23bc; D. Van Ravenswaay 22clb; SuperStock: J. Silver 19br; Warren Photographic: 22cra

All other images © Dorling Kindersley For further information see: www.dkimages.com

London, New York, Munich, Melbourne, and Delhi

Written by John Malam
A catalog record for this book is available from the Library of Congress.
Copyright © 2007 The Book Studio
All rights reserved. First Published in the United States in 2007 by DK Publishing, 375 Hudson Street, New York, New York 10014
07 08 09 10 11 10 9 8 7 6 5 4 3 2 1

Published in Great Britain by Dorling Kindersley Limited.

ISBN: 978-0-7566-2915-1

Color reproduction by Leo Paper Products
Printed and bound in China by Leo Paper Products
Discover more at www.dk.com